THE OGS DISCOVER FIRE

Felicity Everett

Designed by Maria Wheatley
and Graham Round

Illustrated by Graham Round

Language and Reading Consultant: David Wray
Education Department, University of Exeter, England

Series Editor: Gaby Waters

First published in 1994 by Usborne Publishing Ltd, Usborne House, 83-85 Saffron Hill, London EC1N 8RT, England. Copyright © 1994 Usborne Publishing Ltd.

The Og family lived a long time ago in a place called Ogtown.

Grandma Og

Pa Og

Grandpa Og

Mog Og

Ma Og

Zog Og

Bruno

Their home was a cave. It was dark and damp, but the Ogs loved it.

Winter was coming to Ogtown.
The nights were getting cold.

The Ogs huddled around
Bruno to keep warm.

They browsed through brochures of far away places.

When it got too dark to see, they went to sleep.

Goodnight Ogs.

Sleep well.

Stop snoring Bruno!

One Og liked the cold. Who was that?

It would be a
long cold winter
without Bruno.

The Ogs tried
other ways to
keep warm.

Ma got everyone exercising.
But they soon ran out of steam.

Pa asked a passing dinosaur to stand in for Bruno.

But it just wasn't the same.

Grandpa invented a cave warmer. But he couldn't get it going. Why?

Og's Original
Cave Warmer

INSTRUCTIONS
1. Turn handle
2. Pull lever
3. Press button
(will not work
if frozen.)

Suddenly Grandma had an idea.

There wasn't much time.

She fetched her big wooden knitting needles and lots of wool.

She knitted

and knitted

and knitted

and knitted.

10

By the next day she had knitted five snowsuits.

But then she was so tired, that she mixed them all up.

Only one Og had the right snowsuit. Who was it?

11

That afternoon the snow came.

Zog and Mog played
outside with their friends...

...until the snow
got too deep.

Despite their snowsuits, the Ogs shivered. Except for Grandma.

Knitting Pattern

Right Sleeve ☑
Hood ☐
Left Sleeve ☑
Front ☑
Right Leg ☐
Back ☑
Right Foot ☑
Left Leg ☑
Left Foot ☑

She was knitting fast to get her own snowsuit finished before nightfall.

Which pieces of her snowsuit did Grandma still have to knit?

13

Clickety click went Grandma's knitting needles. Her fingers were just a blur.

What's that funny smell?

And where's that black cloud coming from?

Both seemed to be coming from Grandma's knitting.

Grandma didn't notice.

Just then a big orange tongue
licked Grandma on the nose.

It was hot and scary.

It's alive.

15

Now red hot tongues were leaping all over Grandma's knitting.

It was on fire.

But the Ogs had never seen fire before.

They thought a monster had come from nowhere and gobbled up the knitting.

16

And they weren't going to stick around to see what it wanted for dessert.

Run for your lives!

One Og has stayed behind.

Og's Original Cave Warmer

Can you see who it is?

Do something! The knitting monster's got Mog.

Pa and Zog started to throw snowballs into the cave.

They hoped this would scare the monster away.

18

Back came a rock.

It nearly hit me.

It's a message but it's broken.

The message was from Mog.

Can you tell what it said?

19

The Ogs tiptoed back into the cave.

You've tamed the knitting monster Mog, well done.

The snowballs had almost finished off the knitting monster.

This is no monster.

Mog had made an amazing discovery.

She was feeding it pieces of wood to keep it alive.

Where did Mog get the wood from?

They didn't need their snowsuits any more.

Grandpa needed his thinking cap though.

I feel an invention coming on.

What did Grandpa invent?

From then on the Ogs
hardly noticed the cold.

They warmed their
toes and toasted their
muffins by a
roaring fire.

Bruno came back
from the woods.

And best of all,
his fleas couldn't stand the smoke.